#4 HALF PIPE RIP-OFF

Laban Hill

HYPERION PAPERBACKS FOR CHILDREN

NEW YORK

Printed in the United Staes of America.

First Edition

1 3 5 7 9 10 8 6 4 2

The text for this book is set in 12-point Adobe Caslon.

ISBN: 0-7868-1282-6

Library of Congress Catalog Card Number: 97-80195

XTREME MYSTERIES

#4   HALF PIPE RIP-OFF

"Watch this!" Wall Evans called to his friends as he skateboarded down his driveway on Friday afternoon. His muscles tensed as he slipped his back foot behind the trucks and popped up the nose of his board. In a flash, he kicked the board into the air with his front foot and landed cleanly onto an old railroad track for a 50-50. They had found the long iron track in the woods near an abandoned mine and had dragged it out. It was the main feature of the small course they had set up on Wall's dead-end street.

Skreeeet! The music of metal on metal. There's nothing sweeter than a perfect July afternoon when you're skating with your pals. Wall shifted his weight forward and his board went into a nose grind on the iron track. Tiny sparks flew out from his trucks before he kicked the backside of his board to flip it.

As he landed on the pavement, he glanced up at his crew—Natalie "Nat" Whittemore, Kevin Schultz, and Jamil Smith. "Don't blink!" Wall shouted.

His front foot stomped the deck. The tail bounced up, followed by the nose, into a massive nollie at least two feet off the pavement. Wall sucked air as if it would make him lighter, while his heel pushed down on the back edge. The board flipped like a hot cake and landed wheels up.

"Umph!" Wall crashed hard on his hip. The pain shot up his spine to his shoulder. Sucking air didn't work. What goes up, must come down—and not exactly the way he planned. Wall unbuckled his helmet and tore off his knee and elbow pads.

"Tony Hawk crashes and burns at the X Games!" Jamil shouted as he whacked his hammer against the nail he was driving. Tony Hawk was one of the gnarliest pro skaters around. The crew always pretended to be their extreme heroes when they tried a really rad move. They were all in Wall's yard, building a half pipe. After Wall and Kevin came back from the Summer X Games, they were amped to have their own vert. Wall had put together a cool street course with a couple of ramps and a rail, but now he and his friends wanted a really sick ride. Wall had just taken a quick spin on the street course to break up the tedium of the job.

"Tony Sparrow is more like it," Wall cracked. He kicked his skateboard into the grass where it turned over, wheels spinning. "Back to work."

"Not so fast," Jim Romanoff, the postman, said as he came up the driveway in his blue summer uniform of shorts and knee socks. "You've got mail!" He sorted through the stack of letters. "Two letters, in fact, for Walter Evans."

"All right!" Wall loved getting mail. Mainly because he rarely got any. Besides the dorky kids' magazine his grandma signed him up for every year and the five dollars she sent on his birthday, all the mail at the Evans household was for Wall's dad. Since his mom had left the family a year ago, it was just Wall and his dad.

"Open it," Nat said impatiently as she sat back on her heels and set down a saw.

"Hey this one's from the Strut and Jive Summer Skate DEMO•lition Tour!" Wall said excitedly.

"You must've won," Jamil said as he stood on his toes to see over Wall's shoulder. Jamil was a good three inches shorter than Wall. He was a wiry kid with blond dreadlocks that looked a bit like a dirty old shag rug. At twelve, he was a year younger than the others, but that didn't matter to his friends. "Mark is going to be totally bent that you won." A week earlier Wall found out that he and Mark Kirsten were the finalists in the contest to design the logo for this summer's Strut and Jive DEMO•lition Tour.

"This'll make him humble," Nat added. At Hoke Valley Middle School, Mark Kirsten was known for his humungous ego—which made him unbearable to be around.

Wall tucked a loose strand of hair behind his ear and tore the envelope open. He pulled out two pieces of paper. The first was a letter.

They all held their breath.

"And the winner is . . . ," Kevin joked. He had come over the from half-pipe frame, where he was nailing two-by-fours together. His close-cropped afro was speckled with sawdust, like a bad case of dandruff.

"Wall Evans!" Jamil shouted as he read the letter over Wall's shoulder. He slapped his friend on the back. "I knew you'd win."

"What do you get?" Kevin asked

"A two-hundred-dollar gift certificate to Rumble Boards," Wall replied.

"Now you can buy that new deck you've been drooling over," Jamil said as he continued to read over Wall's shoulder. "Wow, and there's even an awards ceremony next Thursday!"

"Next Thursday!" Nat shouted. "Dig that. All the pros are going to be here." She pumped her fist in the air. Thursday was only six days away.

Wall opened the second piece of paper. It was the flyer for the DEMO, and on it was Wall's totally rad drawing—a stick figure with long hair flying all over the place, catching air on a skateboard, and performing a perfect nose grab. He liked the drawing even more now that he saw it in print. A goofy grin spread across his face as he imagined himself accepting his prize in front of the whole town. Everyone was going to know him now—even though he'd only moved to Hoke Valley a few months ago.

"Let's get our half pipe finished," Kevin said. As usual, Kevin was focused on getting the job done and not goofing around. "So we can practice and be primed to ride on Thursday." The DEMO was both a skate demonstration by the pros on the tour and an opportunity for kids to test out all kinds of decks, trucks, and wheels.

"Hey," Jamil said as he snagged the flyer out of Wall's hands. "Brewster Kale is on the tour. He's going to be giving clinics." Jamil glanced at Wall. "You saw him at the X Games, right?"

"We saw Tony Hawk massacre him on the vert," Wall replied.

"Awesome!" Nat responded. "Let's finish this pipe. I'm dying to perfect my nose grind."

"And I can't wait to pop a really gnarly 540 backside boardflip," Jamil added.

"In your dreams!" Kevin cracked.

Then Wall remembered the second letter. He tore open the envelope and froze. It was a letter from his school telling him who his summer school English teacher would be. Shaking his head, he sunk to the grass. "I'm dead. I'm going to have Mrs. Kirby for the rest of my life."

This past spring, when Wall had moved to Hoke Valley, he was put in Mrs. Kirby's English class. This was more than bad. For Wall it was a total disaster. He had spent the last few years being home-schooled. He was used to having input on what he read and what kind of work he did. With Mrs. Kirby everything was different. Wall had to do exactly what she wanted or he was dead meat. Wall ended up flunking English, and now had to repeat it in summer school.

"What's wrong?" Nat asked.

Wall looked up at Nat. He was a little embarrassed to explain to her that he had to go summer school. She almost always got straight As. "Mrs. Kirby is teaching my English class this summer. There's no way I'll pass now." He crumpled up the letter. "She hates me."

"Don't worry," Nat replied. "I'll help you. I did really well in her class. You just have to know what she wants."

"It's no prob," Wall said. "I can handle it."

Nat shrugged. "Whatever." She began sawing a two-by-four.

Wall stood and watched his friends work for a minute. "Hey, guys, let's check out Rumble Boards. I'm going to need help deciding what to spend my gift certificate on."

"But we've got a lot to do," Kevin protested. They were almost completely done with the frame. Then they could start screwing on the plywood.

"I could definitely use a break," Jamil said as he put down his hammer.

Jamil had a reputation for being a slacker, which wasn't completely true. When he got caught up in a mystery, he could be as dogged as any of them. Still, he didn't mind when people underestimated him. He could surprise them that way.

"You could always use a break," Nat cracked. Then she glanced over at Wall and saw how bummed he looked. "But I could use a break, too."

Kevin watched his friends grab their skateboards, and knew it was a lost cause. "Just promise me we'll finish this pipe tomorrow."

"Cross my heart," Wall replied. He kicked his board up into his hand.

"Don't forget 'hope you die,'" Jamil cracked. "Then we *really* know you mean it."

They laughed and skated the few blocks to the center of town.

"I can't believe I won," Wall said as they turned onto Main Street and took a shortcut across the parking lot of the Slopeside Motel.

"Whoa! Hold up crew," Nat said as she came to a stop on the sidewalk right in front of the motel. She was looking at a graffito spray-painted on the cement. But this wasn't just any graffito. It was a copy of Wall's drawing that had won the DEMO contest!

Wall spun around and saw what Nat was staring at. "Who would do this?" he wondered.

"It has to be Mark," Jamil insisted as he looked at the tag. "He must have found out today that he lost and you won. And he knows what your logo looks like because it was posted with his when they announced that you were the finalists."

"You think he'd be upset enough to make me look like a vandal?" Wall asked. "That seems a little over the top."

Kevin knelt beside the drawing. "The paint's dry so it wasn't done in the last hour." He was already examining the graffito for clues.

"We've got to wash this off," Wall said.

"How?" Kevin asked. "Soap and water won't do it."

"Maybe the hardware store has something to remove graffiti," Wall replied. He knelt beside the tag. "It looks like the stick figure was deliberately drawn badly." The tag was both crudely done and backward. The skater in Wall's drawing was riding regular, while this skater was riding goofy.

"Like someone was dissing your drawing," Jamil added.

"That's something Mark might do," Nat suggested. "If he wanted to make you look bad."

"This day has really gone downhill," Wall complained. "First I win the contest, which was so cool I was flying. Then I crash five minutes later when I find out I'm stuck with Mrs. Kirby again. And now someone is trying to get me in trouble." Wall made the whistling sound of a plane falling to earth. "Bam! He crashes and burns!"

"Wait, you guys are jumping to conclusions," Kevin said. "Do you really think Mark would do this? It could be anybody who has seen your design."

"Maybe," Jamil continued. "But it seems like the kind of thing Mark would do. Besides, who else has seen it. The flyer hasn't even been distributed, has it?"

"We should check that out," Kevin suggested.

"Mark's got more of a motive than anyone else," Nat explained. "Remember how he told everyone at school that he was going to win the contest? He's either making fun of Wall or trying to get him in trouble. Everybody's going to think Wall did it."

"Sounds like we've got a mystery," Kevin said excitedly. "Let's do this right and follow the clues."

"Right," Nat seconded. She kicked her skateboard up into her hand. "We should nail Mark, now."

"Not so fast," Wall replied. "Kevin's right. We need to follow our leads first. This tag was painted with white spray paint. The first thing we need to do is track that paint down."

"Let's check out Valley Hardware and see if anyone has bought spray paint recently," Kevin said. "We could wrap this up quickly if we can link Mark to the paint."

"And we can get some paint remover at the same time," Wall said. "I want to get this off the sidewalk before anyone else sees it." Wall definitely didn't want anything or anyone to get in the way of his big moment.

"Let's go," Nat said as they all headed across town on their skateboards.

Valley Hardware was on the other side of Hoke

Valley Middle School. The crew had to pass the school in order to get there. This time of day, lots of kids met on the playground to skate, ride bikes, and play basketball. This afternoon was no different. As they approached the blacktop, Jamil came to a stop.

"Hey, wait a sec," Jamil said. "Check out the new kids." Jamil pointed to a girl with her hair cut short, wearing baggy jeans and a lime green T-shirt. She ollied up onto the chain-link fence in front of them and pushed off. Her board bounced about three feet straight out and flipped. She landed perfectly on it and skated off.

"She rocks!" Nat gasped in awe.

"We saw Brewster Kale do that on the street course at the X Games," Wall said excitedly. "It's called a Brew Twist because he invented it."

"She must have seen it on TV," Kevin said.

The girl rode over to some guy who had just slipped and fallen. She helped him up.

"Do you know them?" Wall asked.

"Nope," Kevin answered. He knew everyone in town. "I've never seen them before."

Nat turned her back to the playground and said, "Don't look now, but guess who's thrashing with Ian Atkins?"

Mark Kirsten was riding his BMX on the far side of the playground. He was a major wide body who handled his bike awkwardly.

When he saw Wall and the crew, he biked toward them.

"Hey, Wall," Mark called as he rode by, "I guess runners-up for the DEMO contest get their designs painted on sidewalks—so everyone can step on them!" He laughed. "That's appropriate."

"You don't know anything, Mark," Nat said in a huff. "Wall won—"

It was useless to explain further. Mark was already speeding back to the other side of the playground.

"He's so lame," Jamil remarked.

"I guess he hasn't gotten his rejection yet," Wall said with a smile. It felt good to have beat out Mark Kirsten, for once. Wall and Mark were the top two artists in their class.

"That doesn't mean that he didn't paint your design, though," Kevin pointed out. "In fact, how did he know about it?"

"Why don't we head to the hardware store and investigate there first," Nat suggested. "Maybe we'll find something that totally points to Mark as the culprit."

Inside the hardware store, the crew went directly to the back, where Tim Johnson, the owner, was stocking shelves. The store was small and tightly packed with all kinds of hardware—from plumbing supplies to nails.

"Mr. Johnson," Jamil said officiously. The crew always let Jamil to talk to people because he had an uncanny ability to get information out of them.

Mr. Johnson stepped off the ladder and smiled. He was wearing a red apron with VALLEY HARDWARE printed on its bib.

"Has anyone bought spray paint from you in the last week?" Jamil asked.

"White spray paint," Wall added.

Mr. Johnson scratched his head as he thought. "Thelma!" he called into the back to his wife.

"What?" she answered in a high, reedy voice.

"Did you sell any spray paint?"

"No."

Mr. Johnson shrugged. "Nope."

"Do you have anything that can remove spray paint?" Wall asked. He wanted to get that tag off the street before anyone connected it to him.

"Nope," Mr. Johnson said again. "But I've ordered some. It's a special solvent that was developed by the New York City subway system to remove graffiti. It'll be in by Wednesday."

"Thanks, Mr. Johnson," Wall said.

The crew turned to leave. But Jamil had one more question. "Is this solvent something you normally stock?"

"Well, no. Someone else was asking for it this morning," Mr. Johnson answered.

"Who?" Wall asked excitedly. "This sounds like a clue," he said to his friends.

"Was it the Slopeside Motel?" Kevin blurted.

Mr. Johnson looked confused for a second. "The Slopeside?" He shook his head and looked at Kevin. "Naw . . . it was your dad, son."

"My dad?" Kevin repeated in surprise.

"Yup, he called first thing this morning and told me

he needed it to clean up his sidewalk," Mr. Johnson explained. He picked up a box and climbed back up the ladder.

The crew glanced at each other. They were all thinking the same thing—Alpine Sports, the store owned by Kevin's parents, must've been tagged, too.

"Thanks, Mr. Johnson," Wall said as they dashed out of the store.

Outside, Nat said what they were all thinking. "We'd better check out Alpine Sports!"

"I'm already on my way," Kevin called over his shoulder to his friends. He had kicked his skateboard ahead and was running to jump on.

Alpine Sports was located on the walking mall that ran for six blocks from Hoke Valley Ski Resort. It was where most of the stores that catered to vacationers were located.

Outside Alpine Sports, Gene Schultz, Kevin's dad, was on his hands and knees scrubbing the sidewalk. His brush swiped across Wall's stick figure skater without any effect. It looked as if someone with little skill had done it quickly and backward, just like the one in front of the Slopeside.

The crew pulled up beside Mr. Schultz and stared at the tag.

Mr. Schultz stood up and dropped his scrub brush in a bucket full of soapy water. "Wall, I know this is your design. But I really hope you had nothing to with this graffiti."

Wall's jaw dropped. "I—I—didn't do it," he stuttered. He backed into the store window. He felt like he wanted to run, but he couldn't.

"Someone is using Wall's drawing and tagging all over town," Kevin explained to his dad.

"There's one just like it in front of the Slopeside," Nat said.

"And the guy who did them can't even draw," Wall added. He pulled the DEMO flyer out of his pocket and showed it to Mr. Schultz. "See. My drawing is different. This one is painted badly and it's done backward."

"I can see what you mean," Mr. Schultz said as he examined the flyer. "I just hope other people don't think you're to blame if this tagger keeps it up."

Wall groaned.

"It doesn't help that the drawing is an advertisement for another sports shop," Mr. Schultz remarked.

"Hey, I just thought of something. Do you think Cyrus is behind this?" Jamil asked. Cyrus McGowan owned Rumble Boards, the sponsor of the DEMO.

"I just can't imagine Cyrus would do something like this. He and I have a great relationship," Mr. Schultz answered as he carried his brush and bucket inside the store.

"Do you think Cyrus could have done it to promote the DEMO?" Nat asked her friends.

"There's only one way to find out," Wall replied as he looked up at the clock on top of Town Hall. It was already five o'clock. "Let's head to Rumble Boards and ask Cyrus how he's using the logo. If it is him we could just ask him to stop. I'm sure he wouldn't want to keep incriminating me this way."

"Right now, though, I think we should keep an eye on Mark," Jamil suggested. "I still have him pegged as the prime suspect."

"And I think we should interview the manager of the Slopeside," Kevin said. "In case he or one of his desk clerks saw something."

"If we go to the playground now, and check out what Mark's up to—" Jamil said.

"We can do a little skating while we're there," Nat finished her friend's thought.

"We have an hour until we have to be back at my house for dinner," Wall said. "Let's skate until then." Earlier in the day he had invited his friends over for hot dogs and hamburgers. His dad was cooking on the grill. "We can follow up on the Slopeside tomorrow when we talk to Cyrus."

"Excellent," Kevin agreed. He skated over to a curb and ollied to tail grind to fakie.

On the far side of the blacktop Ian Atkins was riding down some steps. He ollied to the railing and peg-grinded the final few feet. Besides Ian, the playground was empty. The crew were disappointed that they wouldn't be able to tail Mark, but they decided to do some skating any way.

Nat skated off a ramp someone had left in the middle of the playground and tried to flip her skateboard.

She landed hard on her elbow. "Good thing we're wearing lots of padding."

"And helmets," Wall added. "I don't think I'd try that ramp without them. I'd skip the aerials." He did a balletic spin on the front wheels of his board.

Jamil came screaming across the blacktop and hit a crack. He flew across the pavement, bouncing about ten feet. He rapped his knuckled on his knee pads. "These puppies work!" He laughed. Jamil stood and picked up his board. After that crash he was definitely done for the day. "Hey! Let's eat."

Nat seconded Jamil as she carried her skateboard over.

At that moment, Wall pulled up alongside Ian. "Hey, Ian. S'up?" He wanted to milk Ian for information about Mark. Ian and Wall had become friendly a couple of months back after Ian was cleared as a suspect in the mountain bike mystery.

Ian smiled and stopped. "Just practicing."

"You know, I'm building a half pipe at my house. You should come over and check it out," Wall said.

"Cool! I built a pipe in the barn behind my house. Nobody was using it, so the 'rents said I could," Ian replied. "I've got summer school, but you could come over in the afternoon and check out how I put it together."

"I'm sentenced to summer school, too," Wall replied. "What class?"

"English," Ian answered.

"Me, too. Mrs. Kirby?" asked Wall.

"Yeah," Ian replied. He bounced his front tire against the ground. "If you want, I can be your technical advisor on your pipe."

"Solid! We could use some help," Wall said. "But first I wanted to ask you about Mark. I saw you riding with him earlier."

Ian nodded.

"Is he bent about not winning the contest?" Wall asked.

"Not that I know of. He didn't talk about it," Ian answered.

"How about painting graffiti?" Wall pressed. "Did he say anything about that?"

Ian shook his head. "He didn't say anything. We just hung out."

The gong from the town hall clock sounded.

"Listen. I've got to jet," Ian said.

"Later, dude," Wall said as Ian rode off.

Kevin was standing by the entrance to the playground with Jamil and Nat. "Hey, Wall! We're hungry!"

Wall waved and started to skate over when out of the corner of his eye he spotted a green army shoulder bag lying against the swing set. He picked it up, thinking Ian might have left it. He figured he could bring it to him tomorrow or at school on Monday.

As he picked up the bag, he noticed the word SMUDGE written in black marker on it. Wall had no idea what that meant—he guessed it was someone's nickname, but definitely not Ian's. Then he heard a clanking that sounded like cans banging together. Wall unbuckled the flap and lifted it up.

Inside were two spray paint cans.

"Hey! You guys better see this," Wall called to his friends. He held up one of the spray paint cans. The can's metal casing gave him a chill of excitement. Maybe they were getting somewhere.

Jamil, Nat, and Kevin rushed over.

"White," Nat said as she read the label on the can. "Same as the graffiti."

"Did anyone see Ian leave it?" Wall asked.

Kevin shook his head. "We already know that crime doesn't fit Ian's profile. He's a mellow dude."

"We learned that during the Bear Claw race," Nat added. A few months before, Ian had been a suspect in a mystery surrounding the sabotage of the Bear Claw Mountain Bike Race. It turned out not to be Ian. Since then, the crew had gotten to know Ian a little more and learned that he was a stand-up guy.

"It might be Mark's. He was riding here earlier," Jamil said. He examined the flap of the bag. "Smudge must be his nickname. I mean, he's into drawing. It makes sense that he would be called Smudge."

"You might have something there," Kevin replied. "One thing we do know is that the tags were done with white spray paint and this bag contains white spray paint. This seems too close to be a coincidence."

"Now all we have to do is find out who owns this shoulder bag," Wall said as he held it up. "If it's Mark, we've got him!"

"But let's chow first," Jamil said. "There's nobody around to interview. And besides, I'm starving. I could down ten dogs without taking a breath."

Wall slung the bag over his shoulder and followed his friends home.

Back at Wall's house, the crew lounged around the picnic table as Mr. Evans burned burgers and hot dogs on the grill. He took a few ears of corn still in their husks that he had been soaking in a bucket of water and stuck them in among the coals. A huge cloud of steam rose and Mr. Evans stood back. His glasses fogged up.

"Wall, could you take this?" Mr. Evans asked as he handed the tongs to his son. Then he took off his glasses and wiped them on his T-shirt. "I hate when that happens." He laughed at himself.

"So Wall, what kind of deck are you going to buy?" Jamil asked. They were discussing how Wall should spend his gift certificate.

"I'd love a new deck," Wall answered. "But my trucks are pretty worn down. And I think I'd like to switch to smaller wheels. They're better on the vert."

"Why not have both, a street ride and a vert ride?" Nat asked.

"Not a bad idea." Wall grinned. "Then I could be tricked out like Kevin." The crew was always ragging on Kevin because he had the best equipment. His parents owned a sporting goods store so he got all the newest and best stuff.

"Thanks," Kevin laughed. "I want to be a poster boy for the consumer life. I'm a slave to fashion. It's not the sport. It's the look."

"Not!" Nat replied.

"I can't help it if my parents own a sports store," Kevin said. "If they owned a plumbing store, you'd be ragging me about how great my toilet seats were."

They all laughed.

"Burgers are ready!" Mr. Evans said as he put a platter on the table. "Hot dogs and corn coming up."

Everyone chowed on the burgers. Mr. Evans sat down when the dogs and corn were ready.

But Kevin couldn't take his mind off the mystery. He remembered the shoulder bag. "Let's take a closer look at this," he said. Kevin turned the bag inside out, hoping to find more clues. Except for the spray paint cans, the bag was empty. "I was kind of hoping there'd be a name or address or phone number inside."

"Yeah, something that would conveniently point to Mark," Jamil added with his mouth full. He had just bitten off half a hot dog.

"If only we knew how to do fingerprints," Nat said wistfully. "Then we could match the prints on the spray cans with our suspects."

"Yeah, right!" Wall said sarcastically.

Nat glanced over at her friend. "Cheer up. We'll find the perp and you'll ace English."

Wall gave her a half-hearted smile.

"I guarantee it!" she replied.

Mr. Evans picked up the shoulder bag and looked at it more closely. "I think this is one of those army surplus bags that Bob's Army/Navy Outlet has on sale this week. I remember seeing a picture of it in the paper."

This comment got everyone's attention.

"This could be a real lead," Wall said, suddenly perking up. "Especially since the hardware store was a bust."

"We can check it out tomorrow morning before we talk to Cyrus and the people at the Slopeside," Nat said, already planning their investigative strategy. "And if we do this right, we'll have plenty of time to work on the half pipe."

"I'm stoked," Wall said as he slapped his fist into the palm of his hand.

After Wall's friends left, his dad looked seriously at Wall. "I hate to bring this up, but your conversation reminded me."

Wall groaned. He knew that whatever his dad was going to say it would not be good for him. "Do I get a blindfold and a last request?"

"Not yet." Mr. Evans smiled. He piled the paper

plates into a garbage bag. "But I think there have to be consequences to your failing English this spring."

Wall froze with a handful of dirty paper napkins hovering midair.

"And those consequences are that you must do well in your few days of English or you won't be able to go to the DEMO on Thursday," Mr. Evans explained. "You'll have to earn the privilege of accepting the prize in public. So I'll need a note from your teacher on Thursday confirming that you're doing well."

"But Dad!" Wall panicked. "Mrs. Kirby hates me. It wasn't my fault I flunked."

Wall nervously rubbed his free hand along the weathered picnic table.

"You've got a lot to learn," Mr. Evans counseled. "You're not being home-schooled anymore. You can't just create your own assignments. You have to follow your teachers' rules." Mr. Evans set the garbage bag down. "I'm sorry, Wall, but you have to prove to me that you can do well before you can be rewarded."

The next morning Wall felt better. Maybe it was the warm, sunny, slightly breezy weather. Maybe it was the fact that he had detective work to do. But as he headed for Bob's Army/Navy Outlet, he felt something big was going to happen today—and it was going to be good.

By some strange coincidence, Wall and all his friends arrived in front of the outlet store at the same time.

"Did we synchronize our watches or something?" Wall cracked.

The others laughed.

At that moment, a tall, skinny guy carrying a roll of posters came bounding out of the store.

"Get a load of this guy," Kevin muttered under his breath.

The guy with the posters looked totally hip. His hair was spiked with the tips died white-blond. His eyebrow was pierced with two rings. And his forearms were covered with tattoos of snakes.

"I kind of like the tattoos," Jamil replied. "But my dad would kill me if I got one."

They scuffed up the wooden steps to the door. Inside, Bob's Army/Navy Outlet was more like a warehouse than a store. Clothes and merchandise weren't neatly laid out on display tables or hung on racks. Instead, everything was piled haphazardly in boxes.

Shopping at the outlet was more like a treasure hunt. You never knew what you might find.

"I once got the coolest jacket here," Jamil told his friends. "It was waterproof and as thin as toilet paper, but I swear you could have hung a tank on it. It was so strong."

"What happened to it?" Nat couldn't to remember ever seeing Jamil wear anything like that.

"Oh," Jamil said as he waved her question off. "I lost it about an hour after I bought it. I left it on the playground and I've never seen it since."

"Okay, enough with the touching memories," Wall cut in. "Let's get down to business. Jamil, you interview the cashier while we check out the store for the bag."

"Roger," Jamil replied with mock seriousness.

The guy working the cash register was dressed in full military gear. He looked like a poster for the Marines, except for his ratty tennis shoes. His feet were propped up on the counter as he leaned back in a chair.

"Nice outfit," Jamil said to break the ice.

"Yeah, the boss makes me wear it. He says I got to project the right image," he said as he looked down at his blue jacket with polished brass button. "I think I look like a toy soldier. But hey, he's the man and I need this job."

"I dig you." Jamil glanced out the window and then turned back to the guy. "So who was the illustrated man?"

"You mean that guy who just left?"

Jamil nodded.

"He's some sort of advance man for the skateboarding thing going on later this week." He jabbed his thumb over his shoulder. "He asked me to hang that poster."

Jamil's heart leaped as he looked at a poster for the Strut and Jive Summer Skate DEMO•lition Tour. Wall's stick man was splashed across the top with the details of the demo below. Since this advance man was promoting the DEMO, he could be behind the tagging. Maybe he was doing a little extra advertising.

"Do you know where he's staying?" Jamil asked. He wanted to find out so he and the crew could follow up on this guy. But he needed an excuse so Einstein here would give up the information. If, of course, he had any to give. "Maybe he's got some posters to spare."

"Sorry," the clerk replied.

"Do you remember anyone who bought a shoulder bag maybe earlier in the week?" Jamil continued. "Like one of these?" He pointed to a pile of army green bags nearby.

"I wouldn't know. I just work weekends," said the clerk. "You'd have to ask the owner. He'll be in on Tuesday."

Jamil turned toward the rear of the store.

Kevin looked expectantly at Jamil. "Any luck?"

"Nada," Jamil replied.

"We haven't had any success either, except that the shoulder bags are definitely sold here," Nat said. "We should touch base with Cyrus and see if he knows anything."

Rumble Boards was located on a side street of the main shopping mall in an old Victorian house. The store occupied the first floor and the basement and Cyrus lived on the second floor.

The crew climbed the broad wooden steps that led to the porch. Through the window they saw Cyrus sitting alone on one of several couches in the store, drinking coffee.

"Yo, yo, yo," Cyrus said as they entered the store. "A big congrats, Wall."

Wall grinned. "Thanks."

"You scoping out the place to see what you're going to buy?" Cyrus asked. He crossed his big work boots on the coffee table covered with snowboard and skate magazines.

"That . . . ," Wall glanced around the store nervously, "and we got some stuff we need to ask you about."

"Fire away," Cyrus responded. He patted the sofa. "Sit. Let's talk."

"What are you doing to promote the demo on Thursday?" Wall asked.

"Don't worry. There will be lots of people there to see you accept the prize," Cyrus said, grinning.

"That's not what he meant," Jamil cut in. "We were wondering if you had anything to do with the graffiti that's turned up around town."

Cyrus looked confused. He rubbed his short goatee. "I'm not sure what you mean."

"Somebody's been spray-painting Wall's drawing on sidewalks around town," Jamil explained. "We were wondering if you know anything about it."

"My dad is really angry because it was done in front of his store," Kevin added.

"Ouch!" Cyrus replied. He sank deeper into the couch.

"So who do you think would be doing it?" Jamil asked.

"The only person I can think of would be Tony Gray," Cyrus explained. "He works for the Strut and Jive Tour and just got in town today. He's staying at the Slopeside. But I'm sure he doesn't mean anything by it. He's just into promoting the tour."

"Does he have two eyebrow rings right here?" Jamil pinched his right eyebrow. "And snake tattoos up both arms?"

Cyrus nodded.

The crew gave each other knowing looks. This Tony guy was starting to sound like a real suspect.

Xtreme Athletes
Hawk Soars!

Skateboarding legend Tony Hawk

Ever since Tony Hawk got his first skateboard, a Bahne fiberglass model, from his older brother Steve, he has been unstoppable. At only fourteen years old, Tony became the youngest professional skateboarder ever. Tony Hawk showed everyone the future of skateboarding, a sport he dominates today, having won more vertical events than anyone in history.

Tony Hawk first began competing in the X Games half-pipe events in 1995, and has swept the first place awards in both vertical and doubles competitions. Now he's gearing up for the 1998 Summer X Games in San Diego.

Tony lives in Carlsbad, California, with his wife, Erin, and four-year-old son, Riley.

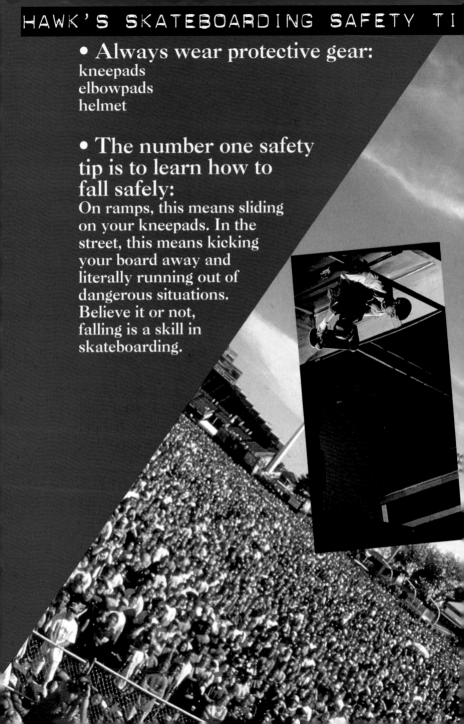

- **Always wear protective gear:**
kneepads
elbowpads
helmet

- **The number one safety tip is to learn how to fall safely:**
On ramps, this means sliding on your kneepads. In the street, this means kicking your board away and literally running out of dangerous situations. Believe it or not, falling is a skill in skateboarding.

A HAWK SIGNATURE TRICK

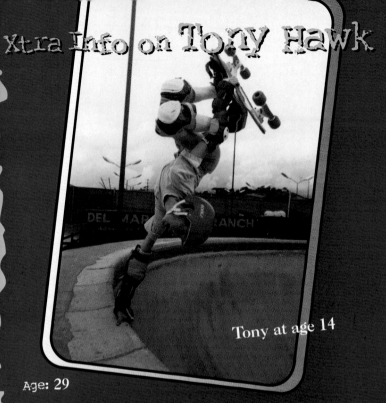

Tony at age 14

Age: 29

Most memorable competition: The 1997 Summer X Games. They took place in my hometown and my family was there—plus I placed first in two events.

Favorite athlete: Michael Jordan, because he wasn't afraid to try something new at the peak of his career.

Favorite skateboard: Tony Hawk Signature model from Birdhouse.

What I like best about my sport: You can create an individual style.

Favorite thing to do on a Saturday: Surf in the morning, play with Riley, then skate in the afternoon and watch a movie at night with Erin.

Favorite pig-out food: Sushi

Favorite movie: *Beetlejuice*

"Do you know where he is now?" Nat asked.

Cyrus shook his head. "Somewhere in town putting up posters."

They made excuses about not being able to hang and took off for the Slopeside. Now there was a reason to check out the motel right away.

"My money is still on Mark," Jamil argued as they hurried to the Slopeside. "He's got a stronger motive."

"And Cyrus did say that Tony just arrived," Kevin said. He was right beside Jamil, while Wall and Nat were following behind. "If that's true, then he wouldn't have been in town when the tags were made."

"But don't forget that we found the shoulder bag at the playground where Mark was riding," Nat said.

Kevin turned and walked backward. "Don't be so quick to blame Mark. That shoulder bag could belong to anyone. We don't know how long it was lying there, and there were at least fifteen other kids hanging there yesterday afternoon," Kevin advised. "We should check with a few of them first before we jump to conclusions."

"I have to admit that right now I'm more focused on passing Mrs. Kirby's class than on who is spray-painting my stick man around town," said Wall. Winning the design contest might be the only good thing to happen to him this summer, the way things were going. He wanted to make sure he had his one moment of glory in all the grind.

Nat patted Wall on the back.

"I'm sorry this mystery is keeping us from finishing the half pipe," Wall apologized. "I really appreciate your help."

"Are you kidding?" Kevin replied. "I'd put aside anything to solve a mystery."

"And we would never let one of the crew get busted for something he didn't do," Jamil added.

At the Slopeside, Nat checked her watch. "Oh geez, guys," she exclaimed. "I'm going to have to bail. I promised to take care of some things for the Bear Claw. I'm sorry to have to ditch out on you, Wall." Nat was deeply involved with the mountain bike racing association. Earlier in the spring she had designed the race course for the Bear Claw's last Hoke Valley race.

"Don't worry about it," Wall said. "We'll fill you in later on any info we get."

"Okay. I'll catch up with you guys at Wall's house," Nat said. "Don't solve everything without me."

As she took off, Wall, Jamil, and Kevin entered the office. No one was inside, so Kevin slapped the bell on the counter.

"Just a sec," a voice said through a door behind the counter. The door opened and an old man appeared. He looked like he had just woken up. The left side of his hair was flattened and the right side stuck straight out. "Yeah?" he said groggily.

Kevin, Wall, and Jamil looked each other. At that

moment they realized they didn't have a clue about what to ask this guy. Kevin and Wall looked at Jamil to pick up the ball.

"Hi," Jamil said. "We noticed the graffiti on the sidewalk yesterday in front of the hotel . . . and . . ." Jamil paused, unsure how to approach this. "And we were wondering if you know anything about it."

The old man went to the front door and looked out at the sidewalk. "Never noticed it before." Then he returned behind the counter. "It's not on my property, so I don't really care one way or another."

"But it's in front of your business," Wall replied.

"It's on the sidewalk. Let the town clean it up," the old man said. He took his glasses off and started wiping them with his shirttail. "Do you want to rent a room or can I go back to my soap?"

Kevin was a bit surprised by this man's response. His dad had been pretty concerned about the tag in front of his store. This guy didn't seem to care at all.

"By the way, we're looking for Tony Gray. Is he in his room?" Jamil asked, changing the subject.

"Let me check." The old man picked up the phone and rang the room. No one answered. "No. Do you want to leave a message?"

"Yes," Wall answered. He gave the man his phone number and asked to have Tony call him.

As they were walking out the door, Jamil thought of another question. "Would it be okay if we asked some of your guests about the graffiti?"

The old man smiled. "Sure, but there's nobody here except ghosts and Mr. Gray. That skateboarding tour arrives on Wednesday and they reserved every room. This time of year the place is usually deserted." He glanced out the window at Hoke Valley Ski Resort, which was just across the street. "Winter's when I'm booked up."

"When did Mr. Gray check in?" Kevin asked. He wanted to confirm Cyrus's information.

"Two days ago," the old man said without hesitation. "I don't even have to look it up since he's my only guest."

The crew gave each other sidelong glances. Cyrus was wrong. They made a hasty exit to discuss the new development privately.

Outside the Slopeside office, Jamil asked, "What's up with Cyrus? Do you think he's hiding something?"

"Or Cyrus could have been mistaken about Tony's arrival," Kevin suggested. He patted Wall on the back. "I think we're in a better position than it seems. We just learned where the pros are staying, and no one has gone nuts about the tagging and gotten on your case yet." He nodded toward the office. "This guy couldn't care less and my dad knows it wasn't you, so we've still got time to solve this mystery."

Wall smiled. "Yeah, you're right. So why don't we work on the half pipe? I need to get my mind off all this."

"Let's jet," Jamil said.

Later in the afternoon the sky began to fill with clouds.

"It's definitely going to rain tomorrow," Wall said as they laid the first panel of plywood on the half pipe's frame. "I want to get this screwed down and covered with plastic before the whole thing warps in the rain."

Kevin pressed hard against the plywood to bend the panel against the curved frame. The half pipe was eight feet wide, six feet at its top, with a curve of twelve feet. It was high enough for Wall and the crew to get some big air, but not too high that they could easily lose control.

Wall drilled the screws through the plywood into the two-by-four frame, four inches apart. He had to press hard to bend the plywood to the curved shape of the pipe. He managed to keep the events of the last two days out of his thoughts and to concentrate on his work until all the panels of plywood were in place. Then Jamil and Kevin began painting the wood with sealant so it wouldn't rot while Wall sat off to the side and began to sort everything out.

He made an effort to see the mystery from a different angle, but he kept coming back to two primary suspects: Mark Kirsten and Tony Gray. Either the tagging was a promotional stunt for the demo or it was a jealous attack by Mark. Whichever it was, if the tagging continued the results would be the same. People in town would blame him.

Mr. Schultz's warning echoed in his mind: the longer this mystery remained unsolved, the more likely Wall was going to be in big trouble.

The rain came down hard and steady. It drummed on the roof of the house as Wall buried himself deeper into his covers. It was Sunday—one day before summer school started. He wanted to delay the beginning of the day as long as possible in hopes that that would keep tomorrow—and Mrs. Kirby—from coming. Suddenly the phone rang.

Wall tried to ignore it, but it kept ringing.

He sat up in his bed. "Dad! Could you get that?"

No answer.

Ring. Ring. Ring.

Wall hopped out of bed, ran down the hall to the kitchen, and grabbed the receiver. "Yeah?"

"Wall? This is Jamil. You better meet me in the resort parking lot," Jamil said over the phone. His voice was tense.

Wall parted the kitchen curtains with one hand. Outside it was pouring. "How about we just meet in a chat room on-line?" Wall asked.

"You've got to come," Jamil insisted. "Somebody tagged the lot three times last night."

"I'm on my way," Wall said before he hung up. He jumped into his clothes and ran out of the house without a jacket or an umbrella. By the time he reached the parking lot, he was drenched.

Jamil called to Wall from the door of the resort lodge. He ran across the parking lot toward Wall.

But Wall didn't need Jamil to show him where the tags were. "This is strange. This one was painted with a brush, not spray-painted. And it's in light-blue paint instead of white."

"The tagger had to use something else," Jamil replied, "since we found the cans on the playground."

Wall pushed his wet hair away from his forehead. "Maybe. It could also mean there are two taggers."

"Come on. I'll show you the others," Jamil said as he led his friend across the parking lot to two more tags.

"Well, these drawings are backward, too and they're all pointing in the same direction. Is the tagger trying to send a message? And does that have anything to do with the change from spray paint to a paintbrush?" Wall asked as he tried to link these tags to the earlier ones, and to a possible suspect. As he watched the light rain land on the crude copy of his drawing, he noticed that the paint wasn't running. It had been dry before the rain began late last night. "The tagger must have done it early in the evening. Did anyone see anything?"

Jamil shook his head. "The resort is closed right now. It doesn't open for summer vacationers for another two weeks."

"Did your dad see anything?" Wall asked.

"No. He wouldn't have even noticed it today if he hadn't had to drop something off at the lodge," Jamil explained.

"I don't get why he didn't use spray paint this time," Wall thought out loud. "It's quicker and easier."

"Like I said, we found his spray cans," Jamil replied. The rain started up again, and Jamil and Wall headed for the cover of the awning.

"He could have bought more," Wall countered.

"What I wonder is why he went tagging twice," Jamil said. "Why didn't he do it all at once? Wouldn't it have been safer?"

"You got me," Wall admitted. "This guy is either a total feeb or . . ." Wall suddenly noticed he could see the front of Alpine Sports from where he was standing. "Follow me. I've got an idea."

He and Jamil ran out into the rain again and headed toward Alpine Sports. They stopped at the tag they had found on Friday. As Wall stood on it, he pointed in the direction the stick figure was pointing. "Look!"

Jamil tried to follow Wall's gaze. "At what? All I see is the lodge."

"No, follow my hand. This tag is pointing in the same direction as the ones in the parking lot. They're like arrows on a trail telling you where to go."

"Whoa!" Jamil exclaimed. "You thinking that maybe all the tags are leading somewhere?"

Wall spun around. From this spot he could now see the Slopeside Motel. "I hadn't noticed this before, but I'd bet that the tag in front of the Slopeside points right in this direction, too."

"Come on!" Jamil called as he dashed down the street.

The rain was now driving pretty hard, but neither Jamil nor Wall seemed to notice. They were hot on the trail of a real discovery.

"You're right!" Jamil shouted. He stood on the tag and pointed directly down the street to the front of Alpine Sports. "But where do they lead?"

"Let's see if we can find out," Wall splashed through the puddles back toward the resort parking lot. "If there are more, they'll be this way. What's over this way?"

"Houses," Jamil answered. "Not much else." Suddenly, Jamil grabbed Wall's arm and pulled him to a stop. Directly in front of them was someone in a navy-blue rain poncho standing over one of the tags. They could see the person shaking his head. Then they watched him move to the next tag and follow the direction it was pointing. He moved to the third tag and looked in the direction that it was pointing. As he lifted his head, the hood on his poncho fell back.

"Tony Gray!" Jamil shouted in shock.

Tony turned and saw them watching him. He smiled

and gave them a wave.

Wall and Jamil splashed their way over to him.

"Excuse me," Wall said. "But you're the advance guy for the tour, right?"

"Yeah, what can I do for you?" Tony said.

"I've been trying to get in touch with you," Wall said.

"You the guy who left that message?" Tony asked. "Sorry, but I forgot to call you back."

"We were wondering if you know anything about these tags?" Wall asked as he pointed to the drawing at their feet.

Tony shook his head and started to laugh really hard. He waved good-bye and headed back down the street toward the Slopeside.

"I don't get it. What's so funny?" Wall looked at Jamil.

Jamil shook his head. "I don't have a clue, except maybe he knows more than he's letting on."

"You got that right," Wall said as he watched Tony disappear down the street. "I think he could be hiding something. This mystery seems to be pointing away from Mark and toward Tony Gray. Now it's even more important that I talk to Ian tomorrow. He might be able to eliminate Mark as a suspect."

Wall couldn't believe he was back in the same classroom that was the site of his spring disaster—with the same teacher who caused it. He slumped low in his seat and kept his eyes locked on his notebook, where he was doodling his stick skater.

Mrs. Kirby was walking up and down the aisles of desks handing out the books they would read over the next six weeks. There were six books in all. One book a week. Reading a book a week wasn't all that bad, but reading a book that Mrs. Kirby chose seemed like torture. Wall just knew she had bad taste. These books were going to be a big bore, Wall thought. As the books stacked on top of his desk, he slid them to the edge without even looking at the titles. The only consolation was that the books weren't thick with lots of pages.

When she was done, Mrs. Kirby stood at the front of the room and cheerfully discussed the books. "We're going to have so much fun. All of these books were my favorites when I was your age." She held up the first book they were to read. It had a dragon on its cover. "*The Ladoon Cavern* is a fantasy about a dragon that tries to take over the earth. All of the creatures of the world band together to fight him. . . ."

A student raised his hand. "Is there a lot of gore and death in it?"

Mrs. Kirby smiled. "Some. You won't be disappointed, Matt."

Wall glanced over at Ian to see how he was suffering these first few hours of summer school. Ian was two aisles over, and he was doing pretty well . . . only because he was snoozing. From past experience, he knew that Ian would be in big trouble if Mrs. Kirby caught him sleeping. So he wadded up little pieces of paper and tossed them at Ian. He hit him on top of his head and the small wad bounced off. Then he hit him on the cheek, but still no luck. Ian was totally out.

Wall was about to toss another wad when he noticed Mrs. Kirby walking up Ian's aisle. Wall groaned and covered his face. He couldn't watch.

Mrs. Kirby shook Ian's shoulder.

Ian bolted upright and tore open a book to look like he was paying attention.

No luck. He was busted. The entire class laughed as Mrs. Kirby stood over him.

"Which of the books is so interesting?" Mrs. Kirby asked Ian.

"Uh . . . uh . . ." Ian flipped the book over so he could

see the cover.

Mrs. Kirby patted him on the shoulder. "Well, whichever one it is, I'm sure you'll enjoy it. I expect a one page report on the first fifty pages tomorrow morning."

The class laughed again.

Wall sat straight in his chair and looked at the front of the room. He didn't want to be noticed.

"And, Wall," Mrs. Kirby said as she turned toward him.

Busted.

"I appreciate your concern for your fellow classmate, but next time just get up and wake him," Mrs. Kirby said. She looked down at the wads of paper on the floor. "I expect you to sweep this room at the end of class today. There's a broom in the closet right over there."

Again, the class laughed. Wall sunk lower into his chair. He was starting off all wrong if he was hoping to get a positive note from Mrs. Kirby on Thursday.

Mrs. Kirby then crossed into his aisle. She glanced down at his page which was covered with stick skater doodles. "You've drawn a really good nose grab."

Wall looked up at Mrs. Kirby in total shock. How did she know about skateboarding?

She smiled and walked back to the front of the room.

At noon the bell rang to end class. Mrs. Kirby handed Wall the broom and left for lunch.

As Ian headed out of the room, Wall caught his attention. "Are we still on this afternoon?"

"Absolutely," Ian replied. "I can ride for an hour and

still get this puppy read." He held the slim book in his hand. "My mom read it to me in grammar school. I still remember the story."

"Rockin'! I'll meet you at the barn in about half an hour," Wall said.

"Solid," Ian said as he left.

Half an hour later Wall arrived at Ian's barn. From outside he could hear loud music and the thumping of kids doing tricks. Bright light, music, and laughter spilled out as he opened the door. It was like entering Oz. The barn was alive with kids. Ian was on the half pipe and a half dozen other guys were standing around watching.

"Sick!" one guy yelled after Ian did a 360 tailspin on his BMX bike.

Ian rolled across the bottom on the pipe and up the other side, where he rose a few feet into the air and landed on his pegs on the pipe's lip. Then he came off the lip and picked up speed with a couple of cranks of his pedals. He flew up the wall and went soaring about eight feet in the air. As he sailed back from the lip of the pipe and over the platform behind, Wall held his breath. This didn't look good. Ian was on his way to splat city.

Ian, however, was unconcerned. He landed perfectly on a three-foot-high box on the back of the platform, then he jumped down and dropped back into the pipe— all without batting an eyelash. He was a genius on two wheels.

Wall wished he had brought his skateboard. He looked around to see if there was one he could borrow.

The other kids had bikes. Wall hadn't really ridden BMX before and didn't want to do it for the first time in front of these kids. They were just too good.

"Wall!" Ian called as he slowed and came off the pipe. "I'm glad you made it."

A kid with a silver bike picked up momentum on the pipe.

Ian and Wall sat together and watched the thrasher for a minute.

"You want to ride?" Ian asked Wall.

Wall shrugged. "Sure, but I didn't bring my deck." He was definitely disappointed.

"I got one you can borrow," Ian said as he went to get a skateboard that was lying next to the stereo in the corner. He handed it to Wall.

"Thanks," Wall said. The skateboard was pretty beat. The metal of the trucks were worn down from too many grinds and the nose of the deck was splintering, but Wall figured he could ride it. "Your pipe looks great. Mine's not as big. I thought it would be too hard to skate something this big."

"Yeah, it's really for bikes, but I know a couple of inliners that come over," Ian replied.

"Rock it!" someone shouted as the biker did a peg grind the entire length of the pipe's lip.

Wall turned from the rider and looked at Ian. "I wanted to talk to you about last Friday."

"Shoot," Ian said.

"After you left I found an army surplus shoulder bag

and I was wondering if you saw Mark or anyone else with it," Wall said.

Ian thought for a second. "Nope. Mark did have a backpack. You know the one I'm talking about."

"Yeah, I know the one," Wall replied. Then he nodded toward the other guys hanging out. "I saw a couple of those guys at the playground, didn't I?"

Just then the rider came out of the pipe and another kid got ready to drop in.

"Hey, Mike, wait up!" Ian called to the kid. "It's Wall's turn."

Mike grinned and backed away from the pipe. "If you're too slow, you blow."

"Why don't you ride and I'll ask around to see if anyone lost a bag," Ian said.

Wall borrowed a helmet, strapped on some knee and elbow pads, and stomped on the board. He entered the pipe and went back and forth a few times to gather speed. Then he popped up high out of the pipe and 360'd to fakie. His wheels screamed as he flew across the well of the pipe and shot up the opposite side. Nose grab and into the pipe again. He rode back and forth with ease, gaining confidence with each trick. As he rode up the vert, he decided to try the most warped stunt he could think of—a 540 boardflip tailgrab.

As he sprung off the lip, he twisted to his left and kicked his board so that it was spinning both around and over at the same time. It looked terrific, but Wall quickly realized he wasn't going to land it. He had lost his board and had to look down to find it. The board was about a foot to his left.

Wall braced for a crash and landed cleanly on his butt on the platform like he planned it. His board slid down into the well of the pipe.

"Fresh!" Ian yelled.

"Sick!" someone else added.

Wall tried to smile, but he couldn't quite pull it off. His stomach was up in his throat.

"Totally lame-o!" came a voice from the stairs. It was Mark and he was carrying his bike up. Wall noticed that he had a backpack slung over his shoulder.

Wall jumped off the platform and came over to Ian.

"Some good news!" Ian said immediately. "Tell him, Mike."

"I think I remember seeing a girl who could do the Brew Twist carrying it," Mike explained. He shrugged. "But I'm not a hundred percent sure." He turned to Mark. "You were talking to her, Mark. Did you see her with an army shoulder bag?"

"Lots of people have those army bags," Mark said, shrugging. He smirked at Wall. "So, you're giving up art to be a private detective, huh?"

"Not quite over losing to me in that DEMO contest, I see," Wall replied. It looked like Mark was going to be no help at all.

Mark blushed. "Yeah, right, as if," he muttered unconvincingly.

"Well if you don't remember, no prob," Wall said.

"I've got to jet."

Ian glanced at Mark. Then he said, "Come on, hang. You rocked on the pipe."

"Later. I promised to meet Jamil, Kevin, and Nat at home," Wall replied.

Outside Wall hurried down the street as he thought about what he had just learned. According to Mike, Mark spoke to the girl who could do the Brew Twist and she might have been the one carrying the bag with the spray cans. Could she be the culprit? Wall picked up his pace. He couldn't wait to bounce this off his friends. Wall turned down Maple Street and passed Rumble Boards— and immediately forgot about his plan. Up in the window someone was standing on a step ladder, painting the image of his stick skater on the glass.

And it was backward!

Wall bounded up the steps two at a time and burst through the door.

Tony Gray was standing on the stepladder with a brush poised to make another stroke.

"Stop!" Wall shouted.

Everyone in the store looked up. Cyrus came out from behind the counter. "Relax, Wall," Cyrus said.

Wall pointed to Tony. "He's . . . he's . . . doing it backward." Wall was so stunned he couldn't get his words out.

Tony came down off the stepladder and looked at the drawing on the window. Then he slapped his forehead. "Of course! What a dope. If it looks right to me seeing it from inside the store, then it's backward outside the store."

"No," Wall insisted. "He's doing it again. He's the one tagging all over town."

"What?" Tony said. "Cyrus asked me to paint the

window. I can guarantee that I didn't tag the sidewalk."

At that moment, Cyrus stepped in between them. "Where have you been, Wall? I've been trying to call you all day. I wanted you to paint your prize-winning drawing on the store window. I'll even pay you."

"Money?" Wall exclaimed. Nobody had ever paid him money to do anything. "How much?"

"Ten bucks," Cyrus said.

"Get me something to wash this off the window and I'll have it done in a flash," Wall said as he grabbed a rag and started wiping off the paint. Wall cleaned the window and painted the stick skater the right way. As he worked, he wondered how Tony could "guarantee" that he didn't do any of the tags. That didn't make sense unless he knew who was tagging. He decided Tony was holding something back—something important.

"Cyrus, I'm done!" Wall called across the store as he stepped back to admire his work.

Cyrus punched the cash register and pulled out a ten.

"Thanks," Wall said as he grabbed it and ran out of the store.

Back at his house Wall spotted his friends riding the pipe. He grinned at the thought that he had his own half pipe. Now he could ride whenever he wanted.

Nat waved from the platform when she saw him coming up the driveway. "How was class?"

Wall shrugged. "Fine," he said. He didn't really want to talk about it. Wall quickly changed the subject by telling them about what he'd found out at Ian's.

49

"A new suspect!" Jamil exclaimed. "If she did do the Brew Twist, she knows skateboarding and about the pros on tour. She probably even knows that Brewster Kale will be here this week."

"But that's not enough to make her a viable suspect," Kevin countered. "What's her motive? I think we need to know more before we jump to any conclusions. We should talk to Mark. It sounds like he knows her."

Wall continued with his story, including how he had caught Tony painting the stick skater on the window of Rumble Boards.

"This might be out there," Jamil said, "but weren't the last tags done with a brush?"

The others nodded.

"And now Wall caught Tony painting his drawing with a brush," Jamil finished.

"That is *way* out there," Nat replied as she sat on her skateboard. "Wall just told us that Cyrus was painting the window and that Cyrus had asked him to do it."

"Hold on. Jamil might have something," Wall interrupted. "We already know that Tony has been in town long enough to do the tags. And we also know that Cyrus gave us wrong information about when Tony arrived. Now, today I found Tony using a brush to paint my stick skater in Cyrus's store. This might be a coincidence, but it's still worth following up on."

"Put that way, it makes sense," Nat replied. "So what do we do next?"

"I'm certain that Tony knows more than he's telling,

especially after he guaranteed that he didn't do it," Wall continued. "He might not be the culprit, but he might know who is. I think Jamil should talk to Mark while the rest of us tail Tony."

"Good idea," Nat said.

"I'm totally up for this," Jamil replied. "Anybody know where Mark lives?"

"I do," Kevin said. "I'll go with you. The fewer people tailing Tony, the less likely they'll be spotted."

At Rumble Boards, Nat checked to make sure Tony was still there. Then she met Wall across the street at the Quick Market.

"He's there," Nat said. "He's drinking a soda and sitting on the couch."

"Perfect," Wall replied. "Now we've got to figure out how to tail him." Wall looked up and down the empty street. "It isn't going to be easy. In all the movies, people are followed on busy streets so that it's hard to spot them. There's nobody to blend into here."

"Hoke Valley isn't exactly Denver, is it?" Nat cracked.

Wall grinned. "I better buy us sodas to use as cover." He disappeared into the Quick Market and returned a minute later with drinks.

"Thanks," Nat said.

Nat and Wall spotted Tony leaving Rumble Boards. They leaned casually against the wall of the building and watched him head down the main shopping district. A couple of blocks away, Tony turned left onto Wilson

Street.

Nat grabbed Walls arm. "He's going to the Bookworm," Nat gasped. The Bookworm was the bookstore her parents owned on a side street off the main drag. She lived above it with her parents and her little sister. "Come on!"

They ran down the street. At the corner they slowed and turned onto Wilson.

Tony was two feet in front of them.

Thinking fast, Wall turned to Nat. "So what's the name of that book you want me to buy?"

Nat smiled, She picked right up on Wall's cover and answered, "*The Old Man and the Sea* by Ernest Hemingway."

Tony nodded as he passed them. "Hey," he said.

Nat and Wall walked straight to the Bookworm and went inside. As the door shut, Nat gasped. "That was close."

"Too close. I think he pegged us," Wall said.

"There's no way you can follow someone in this town during the summer," Nat added. "There's just not enough people on the street."

"Should we try again?" Wall asked.

Nat shook her head. "Let's catch up with Kevin and Jamil. Maybe they found out something."

Jamil and Kevin crossed the Hoke Valley Resort parking lot as they headed for Mark's house. They looked at the tags as they passed.

"Wait a sec!" Jamil gasped. "These tags are all pointing toward Mark's house."

Kevin studied all the tags in the parking lot. "You're right," he said with excitement.

They hurried down the couple of blocks to Mark's street. Mark's house was three doors down on the left. Jamil and Kevin arrived on his doorstep, and rang the bell.

Mark opened the door. "Jamil. Kevin. You guys want to play some video games?"

Kevin looked at his watch and shook his head. "Sorry, we can't stay long. We just stopped by to ask if you knew anything about the tags being drawn around town."

"You got me," Mark said with a shrug. "I haven't got a clue. All I know is they look like Wall's drawing for the DEMO."

"We also wanted to check with you about that skater you were rapping with the other day," Jamil added.

Mark looked confused. "What skater are you talking about?"

"That girl who can do the Brew Twist," Jamil explained. "Do you know her?"

Mark grinned. "Oh, I get it. You're here for Wall. He was asking about her at Ian's." He started to shut the door. "If Wall's such a genius that he wins the DEMO contest, then he can figure out where she lives."

As they turned away from the door, Jamil said, "Wow! He's really mad about losing."

"It sure seems that way. Let's see if Wall and Nat learned anything new," Kevin suggested as they headed back into town.

Standing in the resort parking lot, they caught up with the latest developments.

"It doesn't look like we're going to actually catch the tagger in action," Wall said. He had hoped to have this mystery wrapped up by now.

Just then the clock above the town hall rang.

"It's already eight!" Kevin said. "I've got to run."

The crew broke up for the night, promising to talk if any of them comes up with new leads.

On Tuesday morning Wall entered Mrs. Kirby's class
with a sense of dread. He'd actually read the first fifty
pages of *The Ladoon Cavern* and he found, to his shock,
that he really liked the book. He was so inspired by the
cool world the author created that he drew a detailed
map of the lands described in the book. It looked really
cool. But as he walked to school that morning, he realized that the assignment was actually to write a one
page summary of the book. Once again, he hadn't done
his homework the right way—Mrs. Kirby's way. He
groaned. Why couldn't he just pay attention?

Wall sat at his desk, feverishly trying to remember
the plot. He'd really only paid attention to figuring out
the geography of the lands. It was useless. Mrs. Kirby
was going to nail him for sure.

When the bell rang, Mrs. Kirby came out from
behind her desk, smiling.

Wall cringed. Whenever a teacher smiled it was

cause for alarm. It meant they wanted to trap you in some mistake. He lowered his gaze so he wouldn't make eye contact. The cardinal rule in any class is: don't make eye contact. If you do, the teacher will definitely call on you.

Wall looked up at the clock over the door. Three minutes had passed. Only one hour and fifty-seven minutes to go.

"Walter," Mrs. Kirby said.

No such luck. "Yes, Mrs. Kirby."

"How did you like *The Ladoon Cavern*?" she asked him.

"Well, the wizard was very cool. The wizard, Modolis. That's how you pronounce his name, right?" Wall said nervously.

"Close enough," Mrs. Kirby responded. He watched her eyes narrow. He knew from experience that that meant she was going in for the kill. "Now, how did Modolis and the dwarves set up their camp?"

"Camp?" Wall gulped. He didn't remember reading about how they did it. He could show her where it was on the map, but that was obviously not what Mrs. Kirby was interested in.

Several other kids' hands shot up. It looked like everybody else in class was prepared.

Mrs. Kirby paused for what seemed like half an hour with a tight smile plastered on her face. Then she turned to Ian. "Ian, can you answer the question?"

A surge of relief pulsed through Wall. Now Ian would catch her heat, and he could relax.

Within minutes, though, Mrs. Kirby had zeroed in on Wall again, with another question.

At the end of class, Mrs. Kirby made Wall stay behind.

"Wall, you're going to have to be better prepared for class if you plan to pass," Mrs. Kirby lectured.

"Yes, Mrs. Kirby," Wall said with remorse. "I promise to work harder."

"Good," she replied. "Now I want a one page paper on the dragon's cave on my desk first thing tomorrow."

"In addition to the regular homework?" Wall asked.

"Yes," Mrs. Kirby answered.

Wall gulped. This was going to put a big wrench in the investigation of the graffiti. He couldn't do both. As he walked out of school, he promised himself that he'd work only on homework today. Going to the DEMO and receiving his gift certificate were way more important than tracking down this tagger.

On Wednesday morning, Wall bounced up the steps to Hoke Valley Middle School. He patted the bronze blob that was a sculpture of Mount Olley and the surrounding mountains, and made his way into the building. As he threaded his way through the other students headed to their classes, he spotted Mrs. Kirby standing in the middle of the hall with her arms on her hips. She didn't look happy.

Wall wasn't worried, though. He was ready for class. He had his one page paper and he had finished *The Ladoon Cavern*. He had even liked the book. There were some very cool battle scenes.

"Walter!" Mrs. Kirby barked. "Follow me." She turned and headed straight for the principal's office.

Wall panicked. What could be wrong now? He wasn't prepared yesterday, but she already gave him extra work for that. "Mrs. Kirby, I'm prepared today," he said as his heart raced. "I even finished *The Ladoon Cavern.*

It rocked."

Mrs. Kirby ignored his comments and opened the door to the office. "Inside."

Wall entered the office and sat in the chair facing the desk. The office was empty so Mrs. Kirby took the chair behind the desk. She gave him a stern look. "I'm disappointed in you."

Wall cringed. "But I'm trying, Mrs. Kirby," Wall stuttered.

"This morning I woke up to find that stick figure you were drawing in class painted on the sidewalk in front of my house," Mrs. Kirby explained.

"What?!" Wall gasped. His book bag slipped from his hands onto the floor.

"Defacing my property is not going to get you very far in this class," Mrs. Kirby continued.

"But it wasn't me," Wall pleaded.

Mrs. Kirby raised her hand. "Hand me your notebook."

Wall gave her his entire book bag. She dug into it and pulled out his notebook. All over the cover were his stick skaters doing different tricks. Wall gulped for air as he watched her examine his drawings. His mind raced frantically for ways to prove that he didn't do it. He was coming up blank.

"I swear to you, Mrs. Kirby. I didn't do it," begged Wall. He wiped his hand across his eyes, afraid that he might start crying. He could hear Mr. Schultz's warning that this might happen. He might be blamed. Now it was happening.

"I wish I could believe you, Wall," Mrs. Kirby said. She sighed. "I will expect you to remove that graffiti after class today."

Wall wanted to protest. He considered mentioning Mark and Tony to let himself off the hook, but he held his tongue. He had to get to the bottom of this himself. It was his reputation that was being dragged through the mud. He simply nodded and said he would be at her house after school.

"But, Mrs. Kirby," he said tentatively, "I don't know where you live."

"Don't lie to me," Mrs. Kirby said. "You were just there last night, ruining my sidewalk." Mrs. Kirby got up and marched out of the room. Wall followed her to class. The morning passed incredibly slowly. He couldn't look Mrs. Kirby in the eye and she didn't call on him once. At the end of class he handed her his extra assignment from the day before and told her he'd be right over.

After school Wall went straight over to Valley Hardware to see if Mr. Johnson had gotten any of that solvent in. He had, and it cost exactly what Wall had left from the ten dollars he had made painting his stick skater on Rumble Boards's window.

Wall borrowed Mr. Johnson's phone book to look up Mrs. Kirby's address. He was surprised to find it was actually there: 223 Pinecrest Lane. He thought all teachers had unlisted numbers so their students couldn't track them down and do what he was accused of doing.

As he crossed the resort parking lot and headed toward Mrs. Kirby's street, he noticed that the tags on the pavement were pointing in the same direction that he was going. For a second he thought maybe Jamil and Kevin were wrong. Maybe the tags weren't pointing to Mark's house, but instead to Mrs. Kirby's. But that seemed ridiculous. Maybe Mrs. Kirby's house was on the way to Mark's. He made a mental note to ask Kevin for Mark's address.

When he reached Pinecrest, he saw another tag right at the corner, pointing down the street. Reluctantly, he turned onto the street and walked toward Mrs. Kirby's house. As he looked at the houses to find the right number, he noticed someone familiar walking toward the door of one of the houses in the middle of the block. For a second, he couldn't believe his eyes. It was Tony Gray.

Wall broke into a run. He needed to find out what Tony was up to. If he had anything to do with the taggings. Wall stopped in front of the house and was about to yell out to Tony when he noticed the number above the door—223. Mrs. Kirby's house! Wall thought he was going to faint.

Then he spotted the tag right in front of the walk to the front door. The stick figure was pointing up the walk. As Wall started to follow Tony, the front door opened and there stood the Brew Twist girl!

"You!" Wall shouted as he dashed up the walk. "You!" Wall tripped on a crack in the walk. "You!" he stuttered one more time.

Tony and the girl looked at Wall like he was nuts. Tony stepped inside and the girl started to close the door.

Wall was able to stick his foot in the door just before it slammed shut. "Wait! I just want to talk," he said, trying to speak calmly.

At that moment, another person came down the walk. The girl saw that person through the crack in the door and swung it open. "Brew!"

Wall spun around and standing right in front of him was Brewster Kale, the awesome pro skater scheduled to perform at the DEMO. Wall knew he had found the answer to the mystery, but he didn't know how, and he was still totally confused. He took a deep breath and said, "Okay! Who painted the—"

"Wall!" a voice called from several houses over. It was Nat and she was with Jamil and Kevin.

Now things were getting out-of-this-world insane. "I found the tagger!" Wall shouted to them.

"Who is it?" Kevin shouted back. Kevin, Jamil, and Nat ran across the front lawns to him.

Wall turned back to Tony and the girl. "Who did it?"

The girl smiled sheepishly and half raised her hand. "Me."

"But why?" Wall asked, in shock.

The girl bowed her head. "Me and Tony had a game set up. I left him clues to my aunt's house around town. Then I bet him a skateboard that he couldn't figure out the clues and find his way here before my brother got to town."

"I've been spending the last few days tracking Eloise's trail," Tony added. "And I found you just in time, so you owe me a skateboard."

"But wait! Brew is here. He's in town," Eloise protested.

"Not when I knocked on your door, he wasn't," Tony argued.

"Wait!" Wall shouted. "Everybody quiet!"

Everyone stared at Wall.

"So you," Wall pointed at Eloise, "you painted my drawing all over town as a game of hide-and-seek?"

Eloise nodded. "Yup."

Then Wall pointed at Tony. "And you were checking out the tags because you were in on this game?"

"Exactly," Tony answered.

Then Wall turned to Brewster. "And you're her brother?"

"That's right," Brewster answered.

"Then how come you used two different kinds of paint?" Wall asked Eloise. He was determined to sort this whole mess out.

"I lost my spray paint cans, so I borrowed some left-over paint in my aunt's garage and used that instead," Eloise replied with a shrug.

Just then, Wall noticed the light blue trim on the house, the same color as the brush-painted tags.

"You don't know how much trouble you've gotten me in because of this," Wall said impatiently. "This house is Mrs. Kirby's."

"Yeah, she's my aunt," Eloise explained.

"She's also my English teacher, and she's about to flunk me a second time because she thinks I tagged her street," Wall said.

"Uh oh," Eloise gasped.

"You have to tell Mrs. Kirby I didn't do it," Wall insisted.

"Aunt Jane is going to kill me," Eloise groaned.

Just then, Mrs. Kirby pulled up in the driveway. As she got out of her car, she stared at all the people standing at her door. "What's going on here?" she asked as she slammed her car door.

"Tell her, now," Wall prodded Eloise.

"Um, Aunt Jane. I have to confess to being the person who painted the sidewalk," Eloise said hesitantly.

Mrs. Kirby's lips pressed together. She turned to Wall. "I'm sorry, Wall, for blaming you. I was very impressed with your drawing the other day, but when I saw it in front of my house, I just blew my stack. I jumped to the conclusion that you were behind it. You've given me such a hard time in class this year that I just assumed you were angry with me."

"Thanks, Mrs. Kirby," Wall said, blushing. He was surprised that Mrs. Kirby had apologized so quickly to him. It made him think about how hard he had been on her. Maybe she wasn't out to get him after all. He had to admit that if he had paid a little more attention to the assignments, he wouldn't be in summer school. For the first time he realized that he was just being stubborn, and that if he looked at books Mrs. Kirby's way, he just might learn something. Now as he watched Mrs. Kirby talk with her niece, he realized that she was a real person just trying to do her job. A real person—with a very cool nephew! He still couldn't get over the fact that Mrs. Kirby was related to Brewster Kale.

"We've got a lot of talking to do, young lady," Mrs. Kirby said to her niece as she led Eloise into the house.

At that moment, Wall turned to Nat who was standing there taking in the whole scene with Jamil and Kevin. "Nat, I'm going to need your help with summer school after all."

On Thursday afternoon, Wall headed to the Strut and Jive Summer Skake DEMO•lition Tour. The DEMO was to start in a few minutes with an awesome display of skateboard power. The tour had set up a gnarly street course with a half pyramid, rails, boxes, and quarter pipes that would test anyone willing to go big and mess himself up.

As Wall reached Alpine Sports, he spotted Eloise scrubbing the tag off the sidewalk. He pulled the army surplus bag he was carrying off his shoulder and handed it to her. "Here's your bag back," Wall said. "Why Smudge?"

"It's my nickname because I tend to go *splat* on the pavement when I skate," she replied. She tossed the shoulder bag against Alpine Sports' wall. "Brewster says I'm a smudge on the pavement."

They laughed.

"I threw away the spray paint," Wall added.

"Thanks. I don't think I'll be needing that any time soon," Eloise replied as she returned to her scrubbing.

Wall turned toward Rumble Boards and the DEMO.

"Oh," Eloise called after him. She held up the bottle of solvent. "Thanks for the detergent. It really works."

"Hurry up. You don't want to miss the DEMO," Wall replied and he went down the street.

The music had already started. Someone was speaking over the loud speaker. "These pros will burn their tricks into your memory. First up is Brewster Kale, with his signature Brew Twist."

The crowd cheered.

"A word of warning, folks," the announcer continued. "Don't try this at home . . . unless you're ready to join the Hall of Raw Meat with a cement facial!"

Wall elbowed his way onto the edge of the street course where Jamil, Nat, and Kevin were already planted.

Brewster cracked a sweet frontside ollie.

"Yeahs!" the crowd shouted.

Brewster then shot up the quarter pipe and performed his Brew Twist with pure, raw genius. Next, he picked up speed off a ramp and came straight for a ten speed bicycle. He nollied easily over it, clearing the bike by at least a foot.

"Fresh nollie!" yelled a person on the other side of the course.

Wall glanced over to see who said it, and couldn't believe his eyes. It was Mrs. Kirby. He snaked through the crowd to say hi.

"Next up," the announcer said, "the ollie grab king Mike Winooski. Although Mike works with cement, he's not a mason. Air it out, Mike!"

The ollie grab king rose three feet to do a diabolically fast boardslide on a rail, which he popped into a kickflip.

"Hi, Mrs. Kirby!" Wall shouted above the applause.

"Oh, hi, Walter," Mrs. Kirby said with a smile. "When do you get your prize?"

"After the exhibition," Wall explained.

At that moment, Brewster came over. "I want to show you a really awesome Gay Twist I learned last week."

"Cool," Wall replied. Then, he turned to Mrs. Kirby. "Thanks for the note to my dad. You rock, Mrs. Kirby."

"She's totally fresh," Brewster added.

"Well, I wouldn't have done it if we hadn't had sat down this morning and discussed how you were going to do your work." Mrs. Kirby told Wall. "I'm just glad you weren't behind the graffiti. It broke my heart to think that a student would be angry enough with me to attack my home."

"Not to worry, Mrs. Kirby," Wall replied. "I'm going to work my butt off in your class this summer." He then followed Brewster over to the grandstand. The preparations for the prize ceremony were already beginning.

Wall climbed the grandstand and saw his friends waving from below. He felt like he just landed a totally sick 540 backside boardflip.

aerial-a move that catches some big air on a skateboard-in other words, a high jump

backside-when a trick is performed in the opposite direction from which the skater is going

boardslide-when a skater slides across the lip or rail of an obstacle on the deck of the skateboard between the trucks

deck-the platform of a skateboard

fakie-riding backwards

50-50-a double axle grind (a grind on both trucks)

540 boardflip tailgrab-when a skater rises out of the pipe, spins 540 degrees (1 1/2 times), flips the board and grabs the tail before dropping back in the pipe

frontside ollie-when an ollie is executed in the direction that the body is going toward the outside of the ramp's arc

half pipe-a ramp that is shaped like a U

grind-to scrape one or both axles on the lip of an

lip-the top or upper edge of a ramp or obstacle

nollie-an ollie performed by tapping the nose instead of the tail

nosegrind-a grind on the front truck only

nose manual-a wheelie on the front wheels, usually done on top of an obstacle

ollie-a no-handed air trick performed by tapping the tail of the board on the ground

peg-the 4 inch metal extensions that stick out of the right and left sides of both wheels, used to stand on when doing tricks

tail grind-a grind on the back truck

360-when the skater and the board spin 360 degrees in the air

truck-the hardware on a skateboard that is comprised of the axle and base plate, mounted the underside of the board

vert-a half pipe

If you're looking for suspense on the slopes, harrowing adventure on the half pipe, or mystery on the trails, look no further!

#1 Deep Powder, Deep Trouble

Jamil must nab a mysterious rogue rider or snowboarding at Hoke Valley will be banned forever.

#2 Crossed Tracks

Who's sabotaging the Bear Claw Mountain bike course? Nat's determined to find out!

#3 Rocked Out: A Summer X Games Special

Kevin and Wall are volunteers at the Summer X Games and become embroiled in a sport-climbing mystery.

#4 Half Pipe Rip-off

Wall needs to track down the graffiti fiend who's framing him for vandalism.